The Final FOUR

All About College Basketball's Biggest Event

by Mary E. Schulte

CAPSTONE PRESS
a capstone imprint

Sports Illustrated Kids Winner Takes All is published by Capstone Press,
1710 Roe Crest Drive, North Mankato, Minnesota 56003.
www.capstonepub.com

Library of Congress Cataloging-in-Publication Data
Schulte, Mary E.
The final four : all about college basketball's biggest event / by Mary E. Schulte.
p. cm.—(Sports illustrated KIDS. Winner takes all.)
Summary: "Describes the NCAA Final Four tournament, including some of the greatest teams, players, and moments from Final Four history"—Provided by publisher.
ISBN 978-1-4296-6572-8 (library binding)
ISBN 978-1-4296-9438-4 (paperback)
1. NCAA Basketball Tournament—History—Juvenile literature. 2. Basketball—Tournaments—United States—History—Juvenile literature. I. Title.
GV885.49.N37S48 2013
796.323'630973—dc23 2011048854

Editorial Credits
Aaron Sautter, editor; Kazuko Collins, designer; Eric Gohl, media researcher; Laura Manthe, production specialist

Photo Credits
AP Images: Ed Reinke, 25, John Swart, 22; Corbis: Bettmann, 7, 12, 19; Newscom: Icon SMI/TSN, 9; Sporting News via Getty Images: Ron Hoskins, 8; Sports Illustrated: Andy Hayt, 20, 21, Bob Rosato, 11, 16, Heinz Kluetmeier, 4, 23, 26, John Biever, cover (right), 2–3, 5, 10 (front), 28–29, John W. McDonough, cover (background), 17, Manny Millan, cover (left & middle), 14, 15, 24, 27, Walter Iooss Jr., 13

Design Elements
Shutterstock: MaxyM, Redshinestudio, rendergold

Records listed in this book are current as of the 2011–12 season.

Printed in the United States of America in Stevens Point, Wisconsin.
012015 008725R

TABLE OF CONTENTS

CHAPTER

CHAPTER 1

Last-Second Drama

On April 5, 2010, millions of people watched as the upstart Butler Bulldogs took on the Duke Blue Devils for the NCAA championship. Duke was the number-one team in the nation. The Blue Devils had already won three national titles and were looking to add a fourth. Few people thought Butler could compete with Duke. But the Bulldogs had already surprised many fans just by making it to their first title game.

The Bulldogs took the lead several times throughout the game. However, with only 36 seconds on the clock, Duke held a slim 60-59 lead. But then Duke missed a jump shot, giving Butler the ball and a chance to take the lead.

DICKIE V

The most recognized face—and voice—of college basketball is not a player or a coach. It's announcer Dick Vitale. Dickie V's predictions and comments have been a part of the Final Four since 1979.

Bulldogs forward Gordon Hayward tried a short jump shot but missed. Duke's Brian Zoubek came down with the rebound, and Butler was forced to **foul** him with just 3.6 seconds left. Zoubek made his first free throw to make the score 61-59. But he missed his second shot, and Hayward got the rebound.

Gordon Hayward

Hayward quickly dribbled to half court. With less than a second left, he launched the ball toward the basket. If the three-pointer went in, the Bulldogs would win the game and the title. But the ball bounced off the backboard and rim, and then dropped to the floor. The Duke players piled onto each other to celebrate their victory. Duke won the game, but Butler's gutsy performance showed that even smaller schools have a chance to win the Final Four tournament.

foul—to do an action in basketball that is against the rules

History and Background

Four teams, three games, two hoops, and one title. This is the Final Four, where college basketball crowns its champion.

The road to the Final Four begins every year in November. College basketball teams across the United States have one goal—to win the National Collegiate Athletic Association (NCAA) tournament.

In 1939 eight teams played in the first NCAA tournament. The University of Oregon beat Ohio State 46-33 to win the title. About 5,500 fans watched that first game. Since then the NCAA tournament has greatly increased in popularity. The number of teams has expanded several times over the years. In 1951 there were 16 teams in the tournament. That number was increased to 32 teams in 1975, and then to 64 teams in 1985. Today 68 teams are invited to play in the tournament.

MARCH MADNESS

Each year millions of basketball fans look forward to March Madness. Broadcaster Brent Musberger first used the phrase "March Madness" while covering the 1982 NCAA tournament, and the nickname stuck.

The Kansas Jayhawks' Wilt Chamberlain (13) won the Most Outstanding Player award in the 1957 Final Four tournament.

The NCAA selection committee meets each year in Indianapolis, Indiana, to debate which teams will be invited to compete in the tournament.

Selecting the Teams

Every year in March, the NCAA selection committee picks 68 teams to compete in the NCAA tournament. The NCAA Division I conference tournament winners fill 30 slots. The Ivy League does not have a conference tournament, so the team with the best season record in that conference becomes the 31st team. Then 37 **at-large** teams are chosen by secret ballot to fill out the tournament bracket.

at-large—describes teams selected to participate in the NCAA basketball tournament that have not won their conferences

• MOST INDIVIDUAL POINTS IN A CHAMPIONSHIP GAME •

44	BILL WALTON, UCLA VS. MEMPHIS STATE	1973
42	GAIL GOODRICH, UCLA VS. MICHIGAN	1965
41	JACK GIVENS, KENTUCKY VS. DUKE	1978
37	LEW ALCINDOR, UCLA VS. PURDUE	1969
35	JOHN MORTON, SETON HALL VS. MICHIGAN	1989

UCLA Bruins center Bill Walton

After the 68 teams are selected, they are placed in the tournament bracket. A computer ranking system is used to help **seed** the teams. The top four teams get a number one seed. Each number one seed goes into a separate region. Then each region is filled out with seeds two through 16. In each region, the one seed plays the 16 seed, the two seed plays 15, and so on. The committee tries to make every region evenly matched. Finally, the committee announces the 68 teams that will play in the tournament on "Selection Sunday."

seed—how a team is ranked based on the team's region and conference

Advancing through the Tournament

Teams have to travel a tough road to make it to the championship game. The first round of the tournament is called the First Four. These four games feature the last four at-large teams and the last four conference winners. The winners of the First Four games move on to the second round of 32 games. The winning teams then move on to the third round of 16 games.

After the third round, only 16 teams are left. These teams move on to the regional semifinals, or Sweet 16. The Sweet 16 winners advance to the regional finals, which are known as the Elite Eight. From there one team from each region emerges to make up the Final Four. During the finals weekend, the regional winners face off in two games. The final two winners then battle each other in the championship game for the national title.

George Mason Patriots forward Will Thomas

NO NUMBER ONES

There have been three times when no number one seeds made it to the Final Four. In 1980 the Final Four teams were Louisville (2), Iowa (5), Purdue (6), and UCLA (8). In 2006 the teams included UCLA (2), Florida (3), LSU (4), and George Mason (11). In 2011, Connecticut (3), Kentucky (4), Butler (8), and Virginia Commonwealth (11) all made it to the Final Four.

In 2011 the Connecticut Huskies beat the Butler Bulldogs 53-41 to win the championship.

• MOST TEAM POINTS • IN A CHAMPIONSHIP GAME

Points	Team	Year
103	UNLV	1990
98	UCLA	1964
94	UCLA	1978
92	LASALLE	1954
92	UCLA	1969
92	UCLA	1975

Famous Dynasties

CHAPTER 2

Making it to the Final Four takes teamwork, skill, and good coaching. Repeating that success can be a difficult challenge. But sometimes a school finds success year after year to become a **dynasty**.

John Wooden's Bruins

Coach John Wooden was a legend among college basketball coaches. During 27 seasons under Wooden, the University of California-Los Angeles (UCLA) Bruins won 10 national titles. The school also had four undefeated seasons.

One of UCLA's best players was Lew Alcindor. Later known as Kareem Abdul-Jabbar, Alcindor started for the Bruins in 1966. He scored 56 points in his first game. The Bruins won the championship each of the three years Alcindor was on the team. He was also the only player in NCAA history to be named the tournament's Most Outstanding Player three times.

Lew Alcindor

dynasty—a team that wins multiple championships in a period of several years

After Alcindor left the team, Wooden and the Bruins continued winning. They brought home the title the next two years. In 1972 UCLA had another legendary center in Bill Walton. The Bruins again won the championship in 1972 and 1973, setting an incredible record with seven titles in a row. In the 1973 title game, Walton made an amazing 21 of 22 shots to lead UCLA over Memphis State 87-66.

John Wooden

MOST TEAM CHAMPIONSHIPS

UCLA	11
KENTUCKY	8
INDIANA	5
NORTH CAROLINA	5
DUKE	4
KANSAS	3
CONNECTICUT	3

Bobby Knight's Hoosiers

After Wooden retired, Bobby Knight and the Indiana Hoosiers became the team to beat. The Hoosiers went 32–0 and won the championship in 1976. No men's team has gone undefeated since then. Through 29 seasons, Knight coached teams to five Final Four appearances and brought home three titles.

Indiana Hoosiers guard Steve Alford (12) takes a shot against Syracuse in 1987.

Perhaps the most exciting game of Knight's career was the championship game against the Syracuse Orangemen in 1987. It was a hard-fought game. The two teams traded the lead several times. With less than 30 seconds left, Indiana was down by one point, 73-72.

After Syracuse missed a free throw, the Hoosiers got the ball back. Knight had already decided that the team's best shooter, guard Steve Alford, should take the last shot. But Syracuse's strong defense kept the ball away from Alford. Instead, guard Keith Smart decided to take the shot himself. His long jump shot swished through the net with only four seconds left on the clock. Syracuse had one second left to try a desperation shot, but the Hoosiers **intercepted** the in-bounds pass for a thrilling 74-73 victory.

Bobby Knight

THE SHOT

Keith Smart's game-winning score is known as "The Shot" by many fans. It is one reason why some people feel the 1987 NCAA title game was the greatest game in tournament history.

intercept—to catch a pass made by an opposing player

Dominant Teams

Rivalries often stretch across the country between teams. One of the most intense rivalries in the NCAA exists between two teams that are only 8 miles (13 kilometers) apart.

The University of North Carolina at Chapel Hill is a short drive from Duke University in Durham, North Carolina. The two schools have won a total of nine NCAA titles.

rivalry—a fierce feeling of competition between two teams

Dean Smith coached the UNC Tar Heels for 36 years (1961–1997). His teams won two national titles in 11 appearances in the Final Four. Coach Roy Williams added two more championships to the Tar Heels' legacy in 2005 and 2009.

On December 29, 2010, Duke coach Mike Krzyzewski (sha-SHEF-skee) won his 880th game to pass Dean Smith's record of 879 wins. Krzyzewski has coached Duke for more than 30 years. After his 903rd victory on November 15, 2011, he passed Bobby Knight to become the winningest coach in NCAA history. The Duke Blue Devils and "Coach K" have won four titles in 11 trips to the Final Four.

Mike Krzyzewski

MOST CHAMPIONSHIPS BY COACH

	Coach	Years
10	JOHN WOODEN, UCLA	1964, 1965, 1967, 1968, 1969, 1970, 1971, 1972, 1973, 1975
4	ADOLPH RUPP, KENTUCKY	1948, 1949, 1951, 1958
4	MIKE KRZYZEWSKI*, DUKE	1991, 1992, 2001, 2010
3	BOBBY KNIGHT, INDIANA	1976, 1981, 1987
3	JIM CALHOUN*, CONNECTICUT	1999, 2004, 2011

*CURRENTLY ACTIVE

Buzzer-Beaters and Upsets

The Final Four has featured buzzer-beating shots, incredible upsets, and unlikely heroes. Each game provides a chance for an **underdog** to pull off an amazing victory.

Kentucky Wildcats forward Tommy Kron

CHAPTER 3

Underdogs Win

In 1966 the title game featured the Texas Western Miners against the Kentucky Wildcats. But the importance of the 1966 title went beyond the game itself. Kentucky coach Adolph Rupp refused to recruit African-American players. People weren't sure what to expect when the all-white Wildcat team took the court against the all-black Texas Western starters.

underdog—a team that is not expected to win a competition

Led by guard Bobby Joe Hill, the Miners were a quick team. Miners coach Don Haskins used his players' speed to run a high-pressure defense. Time after time, Hill stole the ball and took it down the court for a layup. Other times, he'd pass it to his teammates for a rim-shaking dunk.

At halftime the Miners were ahead 34-31. In the second half, Kentucky kept the game close with crisp passing and outside shots. With 10 minutes left, the Miners were up by only two points. The Wildcats had a chance to tie the score three times, but they missed all three shots.

The game finally came down to free throws. Kentucky had to keep committing fouls to get the ball. But Texas Western made 28 of 34 free throws to stay ahead of Kentucky. When the clock ran out, the Miners had upset Rupp's Wildcats 72-65.

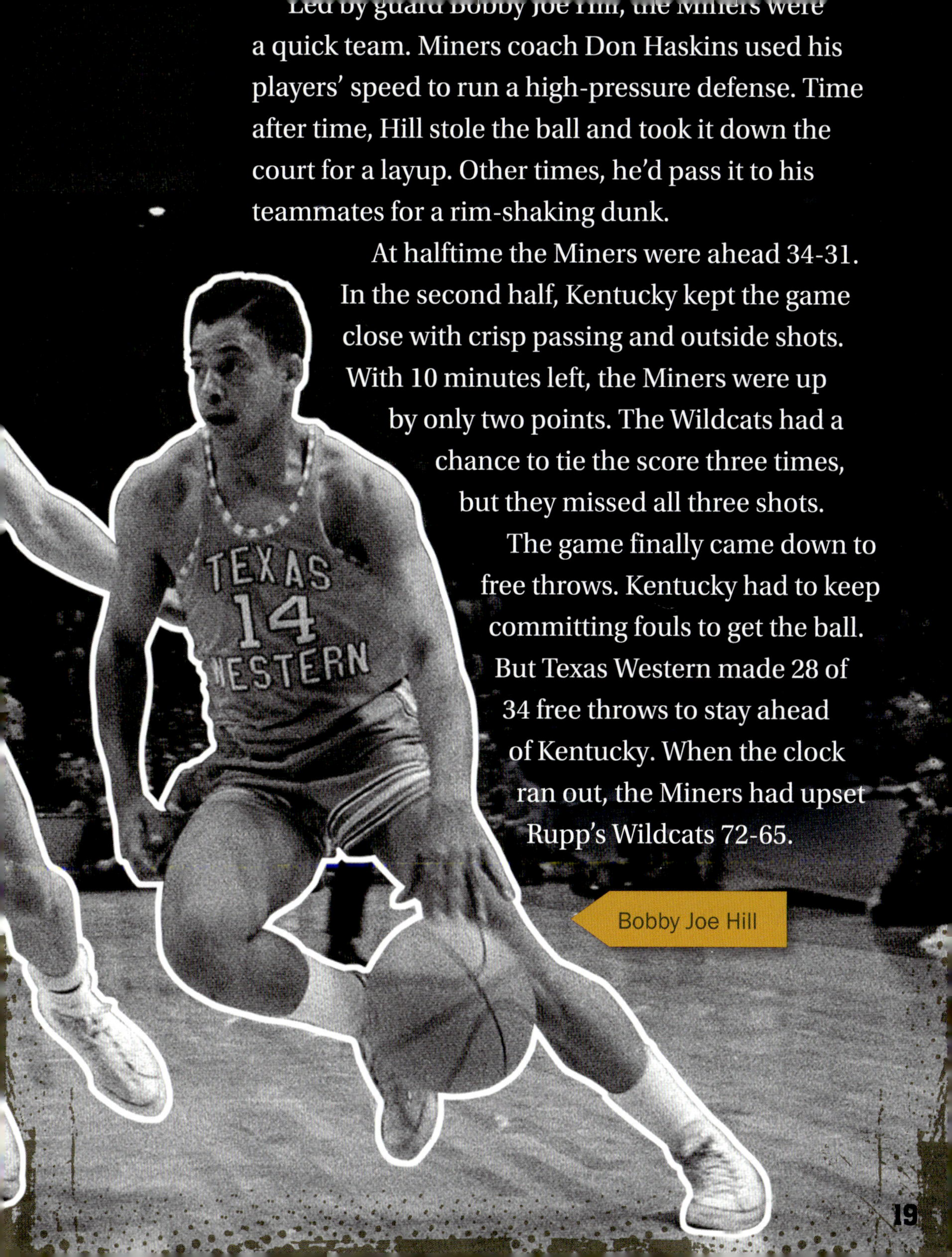

Bobby Joe Hill

Dunking Cougars Blocked

In 1983 few people thought North Carolina State would be a threat. As a six seed, the Wolfpack were big underdogs against the number one ranked Houston Cougars. Led by Hakeem Olajuwon and Clyde Drexler, the Cougars called themselves "Phi Slamma Jamma" because of their amazing dunks. N.C. State coach Jim Valvano knew his team had to stop Houston's high-flying offense to win. During the first half, the Wolfpack played amazing defense and didn't allow Houston to score a single dunk.

But in the second half, the Cougars came out scoring big. Houston eventually tied the score at 52-52. With time running out, N.C. State's Dereck Whittenburg took a desperate shot from 30 feet (9 meters) out. The ball fell short of the basket, but teammate Lorenzo Charles grabbed it in mid-air. He slammed it through the hoop as the buzzer went off. N.C. State won 54-52. Coach Jim Valvano sprinted around the court with his arms in the air to celebrate his team's amazing last-second win.

After winning the title, some Wolfpack players celebrated by climbing onto the basketball rim to wave to the fans.

Dereck Whittenburg (25) scored 14 points for N.C. State in the 1983 NCAA title game.

Low Seed Wins

Two years after N.C. State's amazing title run, an even lower-seeded team took the tournament by surprise. Villanova was the eighth seed in the Southeast Region. The Wildcats beat four higher-seeded teams to get to the title game against Georgetown.

Georgetown's Patrick Ewing (rear) attempts to block a shot by Villanova's Harold Pressley.

Few people thought Villanova had a chance of winning. The Georgetown Hoyas were a number one seed and had won the championship the year before. They were also led by star center Patrick Ewing.

When Villanova's defense focused on stopping Ewing, Georgetown fired up their outside shooters. But the Hoyas couldn't beat Villanova's record-setting 78 percent shooting. The Wildcats won 66-64 in one of the biggest upsets in championship history. Even Georgetown had to respect the Wildcats' amazing shooting. The Hoyas gave Villanova a standing ovation as the Wildcats received the trophy.

Michael Jordan

ALL-TIME STARS

In 1988 the NCAA chose its All-Time Tournament Team. The "starting five" included: Wilt Chamberlain (Kansas, 1957), Lew Alcindor (UCLA, 1967, 1968, 1969), Larry Bird (Indiana State, 1979), Earvin "Magic" Johnson (Michigan State, 1979), and Michael Jordan (North Carolina, 1982).

Wild Moments and Big Blunders

Not all of the memorable moments in the Final Four are good. Bad passes, missed shots, and other small mistakes have often sent teams home in defeat.

The Time-Out Game

Michigan's All-American Chris Webber is well-known by many fans. But he's usually not remembered for the 23 points he scored in the 1993 championship game. Instead, Webber is often remembered for his mental mistake that may have cost his team the title.

Michigan trailed North Carolina by just two points with 20 seconds left. One basket could have tied the game at 73. Webber grabbed a rebound and dribbled down the court, but he was quickly trapped by Tar Heel players. Webber called a timeout. This is normally a smart move to keep opponents from getting the ball. However, the Wolverines didn't have any timeouts left.

Chris Webber

CHAPTER

Webber's mistake cost Michigan a technical foul. The Tar Heels were given two free throws and the ball. They made the shots and then scored another basket. The Wolverines couldn't overcome Webber's blunder. The Tar Heels won the title game 77-71.

Michigan Wolverines guard Jimmy King

North Carolina Tar Heels guard Derrick Phelps

TOP TEAMS

The top two ranked teams have played each other in the title game only eight times. In those games, the number two team won the title five times. The most recent was in 2005 when North Carolina beat Illinois 75-70.

Brown's Bad Pass

The 1982 championship game featured two teams with a lot of history—North Carolina and Georgetown. The head coaches, Dean Smith and John Thompson, were friends. Both teams had rising stars in their lineups. The Tar Heels had future superstar Michael Jordan, and Patrick Ewing played for the Hoyas.

The game had two wild moments. With 30 seconds to go in the game, Georgetown was closely guarding the Tar Heels' main shooters. North Carolina got the ball to Jordan instead. He calmly hit a jump shot from the side to put the Tar Heels ahead 63-62.

Georgetown got the ball back with plenty of time to score. But then guard Fred Brown made a huge mistake. He threw the ball right to North Carolina forward James Worthy. Worthy quickly ran the ball down the court before being fouled with two seconds left. After he missed his two free throw shots, Georgetown grabbed the rebound and threw up a final desperate shot. But the ball fell short. The Tar Heels held on to win and gave coach Smith his first national title.

James Worthy

ONE LONG GAME

The longest championship game was played in 1957. It took North Carolina three overtime periods to beat Kansas 54-53.

Kansas Buzzer Beater

The 2008 title game had one of the most dramatic buzzer-beaters in tournament history. With two minutes to go, the Memphis Tigers had a nine-point lead over the Kansas Jayhawks. But Kansas inched back to come within 3 points.

With 3.8 seconds left on the clock, Kansas guard Mario Chalmers launched a three-point shot. The crowd in San Antonio went wild as the ball went through the hoop. The game was tied 63-63 and going to overtime.

Mario Chalmers' (15) amazing game-saving shot in the 2008 championship game was one of the most dramatic in NCAA tournament history.

The Jayhawks were fired up. They scored the first six points in the extra period. Memphis was out of steam, and Kansas went on to win 75-68. It was the first title for Kansas in 20 years.

Nobody knows which team will be crowned as champions from year to year. It might be a school that is part of a legendary dynasty. Or it could be an underdog team that battles its way through the bracket to claim the title. NCAA fans will keep watching and cheering as their favorite teams try to reach the Final Four.

A FINAL FOUR FIRST

The first time all four number one seeds met in the Final Four happened in 2008. They were Kansas, Memphis, North Carolina, and UCLA.

GLOSSARY

at-large (AT-LARJ)—describes teams selected to participate in the NCAA basketball tournament that have not won their conferences

bracket (BRAK-it)—a way to organize teams in a tournament; as teams win they advance through the bracket to the championship game

dynasty (DYE-nuh-stee)—a team that wins multiple championships in a period of several years

foul (FOUL)—to do an action in basketball that is against the rules; pushing and tripping are fouls

intercept (in-tur-SEPT)—to catch a pass made by an opposing player

rebound (REE-bound)—to gain possession of the basketball after a missed shot

rivalry (RYE-vul-ree)—intense competition between teams

seed (SEED)—how a team is ranked in the NCAA tournament, based on the team's region and conference

tournament (TUR-nuh-muhnt)—a series of games between several teams, ending in one winner

underdog (UN-duhr-dawg)—a team that is not expected to win a competition

READ MORE

Bekkering, Annalise. *NCAA Basketball Championship.* Sporting Championships. New York: Weigl Publishers Inc., 2009.

LeBoutillier, Nate. *The Best of Everything Basketball Book.* All-Time Best of Sports. Mankato, Minn.: Capstone Press, 2011.

Monnig, Alex. *North Carolina Tar Heels.* Inside College Basketball. Minneapolis: ABDO Pub. Company, 2012.

INTERNET SITES

FactHound offers a safe, fun way to find Internet sites related to this book. All of the sites on FactHound have been researched by our staff.

Here's all you do:

Visit *www.facthound.com*

Type in this code: 9781429665728

WWW.FACTHOUND.COM®

INDEX